STAR WARS™
THE
MANDALORIAN
The Adventures of Din Djarin

Penguin Random House

DK
Senior Editor Matt Jones
Project Art Editor Stefan Georgiou
Production Editor Marc Staples
Senior Production Controller Mary Slater
Managing Editor Emma Grange
Managing Art Editor Vicky Short
Publishing Director Mark Searle

Reading Consultant Barbara Marinak

For Lucasfilm
Editor Jennifer Pooley
Creative Director, Publishing
Michael Siglain
Art Director Troy Alders
Story Group Leland Chee, Pablo Hidalgo,
and Kate Izquierdo
Creative Art Manager Phil Szostak
Asset Management Chris Argyropoulos,
Gabrielle Levenson, Bryce Pinkos,
Elinor De La Torre, Sarah Williams,
Jackey Cabrera, Nick Miano, Allison Bird,
and Michael Trobiani
Photographers François Duhamel, Nicola
Goode, Justin Lubin, and Melinda Sue Gordon

DK would like to thank Chelsea Alon at
Disney; and Julia March and Kayla Dugger
for proofreading.

First American Edition, 2024
Published in the United States by
DK Publishing
1745 Broadway, 20th Floor, New York,
NY 10019

Page design copyright © 2024
Dorling Kindersley Limited
DK, a Division of Penguin
Random House LLC

A catalog record for this book
is available from the Library of Congress.
ISBN 978-0-7440-9217-2 (Paperback)
ISBN 978-0-7440-9218-9 (Hardcover)

DK books are available at special discounts when purchased
in bulk for sales promotions, premiums, fund-raising, or educational use.
For details, contact: DK Publishing Special Markets,
1745 Broadway, 20th Floor, New York, NY 10019
SpecialSales@dk.com

Printed and bound in China

www.dk.com
www.starwars.com

MIX
Paper | Supporting
responsible forestry
FSC™ C018179

This book was made with Forest
Stewardship Council™ certified
paper—one small step in DK's
commitment to a sustainable future.
For more information go to
www.dk.com/our-green-pledge

The Adventures of Din Djarin

Written by Matt Jones

Contents

Meet Din Djarin

Din Djarin is a Mandalorian bounty hunter.
He is very brave and looks after his friends.
Din Djarin goes on many adventures.
Din Djarin looks after his son, Grogu.

Grogu

What is a Mandalorian?

Mandalorians are a group of people who come from the planet Mandalore. They are famous for being powerful warriors. Most Mandalorians wear suits of armor. Some Mandalorians disagree on what rules are important to follow as a Mandalorian.

Din Djarin's armor

Din Djarin's suit of armor protects him. It has many built-in gadgets such as a flamethrower and a jetpack. His suit is made of a special metal called beskar. This metal is very rare. Beskar only comes from the planet Mandalore.

Helmet

Jetpack

Cape

What is a bounty hunter?

Bounty hunters are paid to track people down across the galaxy. Some bounty hunters are members of the Bounty Hunters Guild. Bounty hunters often find themselves in dangerous situations.

Cad Bane

Riot Mar

Krrsantan

The galaxy

A galaxy is a group of stars and planets. Din Djarin lives in a big galaxy that is far, far away. Din Djarin visits many different planets on his adventures.

Tatooine

Mandalore

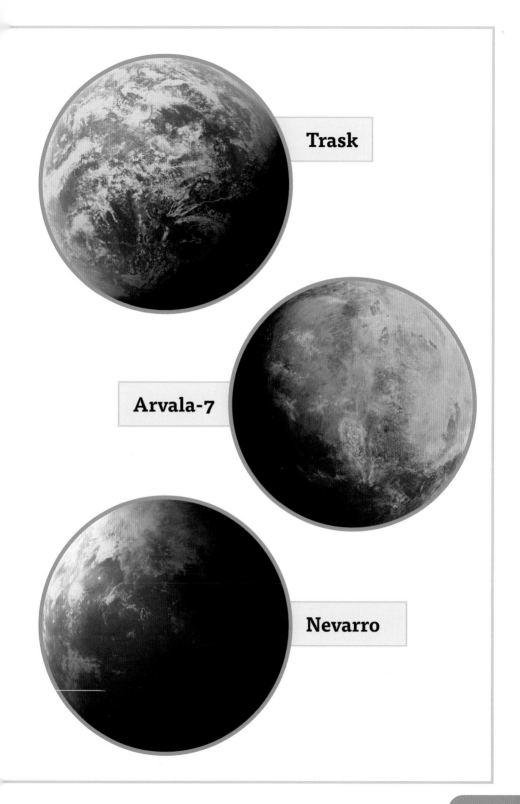

Trask

Arvala-7

Nevarro

The *Razor Crest*

The *Razor Crest* is Din Djarin's starship.
He pilots the starship around the galaxy.
The ship has a cockpit, a cargo hold,
a bedroom, and even a toilet!

Engine

Cockpit

Grogu

Grogu is Din Djarin's adopted son.
Grogu is 50 years old, but he is still
a child. His species takes a long time
to grow up! Grogu can use the Force to
do many amazing things. He can heal
wounds and jump really high into the air.

**Grogu uses a hover pram
to move around.**

The Armorer

The Armorer is a smart Mandalorian.
She is very skilled at making
Mandalorian weapons and armor.
The Armorer is an important member
of the Children of the Watch.
The Children of the Watch are a group
of Mandalorians. They believe that
they should never take their helmets
off in front of others. Din Djarin is also
a member of the Children of the Watch.

Mudhorn

The mudhorn is a species of creature found on the planet Arvala-7. Each mudhorn has a single large horn on their head. Mudhorns use these horns to dig nests into the muddy canyons of Arvala-7. Din Djarin and Grogu defeat a mudhorn on the desert planet.

**Din Djarin is holding
a mudhorn egg.**

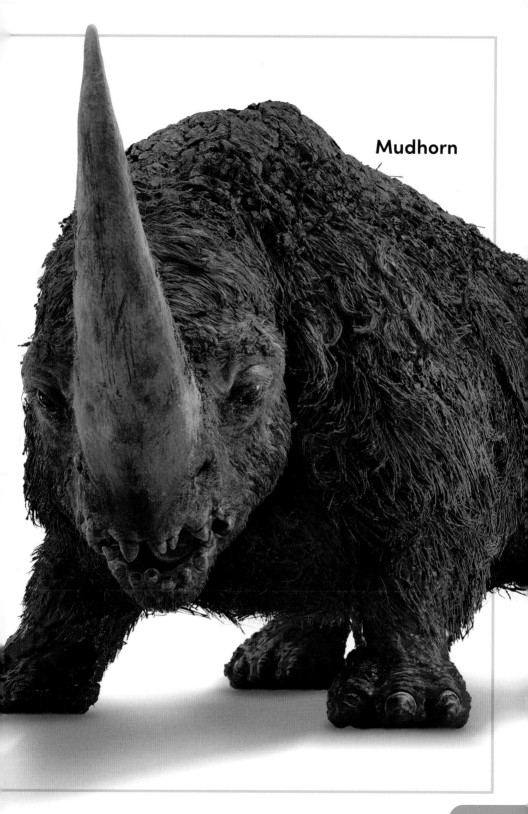

Mudhorn

A clan of two

The Armorer decides that Din Djarin can start his own Mandalorian clan. A Mandalorian clan is a small group of Mandalorians that are like a family. The Armorer names Din Djarin's clan after the mudhorn creature. Din Djarin and Grogu become members of Clan Mudhorn.

Din Djarin's allies

Din Djarin visits many worlds and makes many allies. Kuiil is an expert at fixing droids and vehicles. Fennec Shand and Koska Reeves are great in battle. Carson Teva is a skilled starfighter pilot.

Kuiil

Fennec Shand

Koska Reeves

Carson Teva

Greef Karga

Greef Karga used to lead the Bounty Hunters Guild on the planet Nevarro. Now Greef is the high magistrate of that world. A high magistrate looks after a planet and the people who live there. Din Djarin and Greef are very good friends. Greef likes to give presents to Grogu.

IG-11

IG-11 is one of Din Djarin's allies. He is a droid. IG-11 likes to care for and protect others. IG-11 saves his friends from being captured on the planet Nevarro, but he is badly damaged. Din Djarin finds the parts needed to repair IG-11. The droid then starts working again and decides to help protect Nevarro.

Peli Motto

Peli Motto is a mechanic. She lives in a city called Mos Eisley on the planet Tatooine. She runs a docking bay where ships can park and be repaired. Peli is good friends with Din Djarin and Grogu. She helps Din Djarin find a new ship after the *Razor Crest* is destroyed.

Din Djarin's Naboo N-1 starfighter

The *Razor Crest* is destroyed, so Din Djarin needs a new starship. Din Djarin buys an N-1 starfighter from Peli Motto. She helps Din Djarin repair the ship. These shiny ships are created on the planet Naboo. Din Djarin's N-1 starfighter can fly very fast. Grogu really enjoys the speedy ship!

Engine

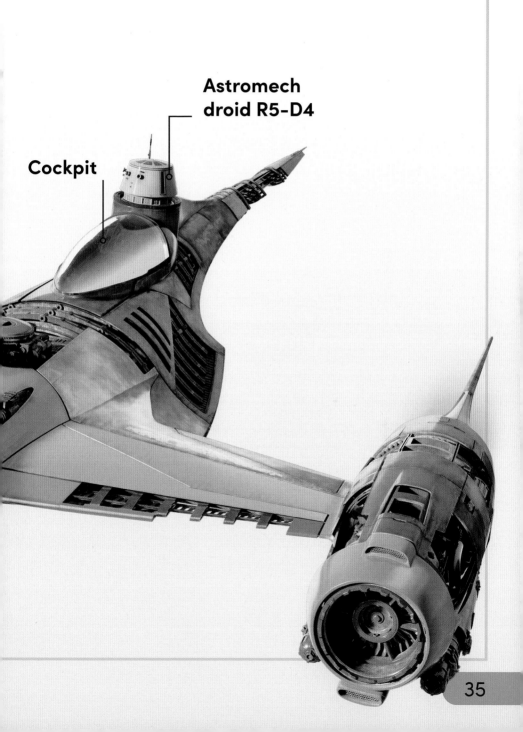

Astromech droid R5-D4

Cockpit

Boba Fett

Boba Fett is a bounty hunter. He wears Mandalorian armor made of beskar. Boba's armor was stolen, but Din Djarin finds it and returns it to him. Boba and Din Djarin help each other out.

R5-D4

R5-D4 is an astromech droid. He knows starfighter pilot Carson Teva. R5-D4 now works for Din Djarin. The droid flies with Din Djarin in his N-1 starfighter.
R5-D4 visits Mandalore with Din Djarin and is very helpful and brave.

Moff Gideon

Moff Gideon is a tough leader.
He defeated Mandalore's leader,
Bo-Katan Kryze, and took over the planet.
Many Mandalorians do not like Moff
Gideon. Moff Gideon decides to kidnap
Grogu. Luckily, Din Djarin comes to the
rescue and saves Grogu. Moff Gideon
has a secret base on Mandalore.

Bo-Katan Kryze

Bo-Katan Kryze used to rule over Mandalore, but Moff Gideon forced her to leave her home. She helps Din Djarin and Grogu on the planet Trask. Din Djarin and Grogu then help her defeat Moff Gideon and destroy his base on Mandalore.

**Bo-Katan, Din Djarin, and
Grogu are good friends.**

New adventures

After Bo-Katan Kryze defeats Moff Gideon, the Mandalorians can return to Mandalore. Din Djarin decides to start protecting others. Din Djarin and Grogu then visit

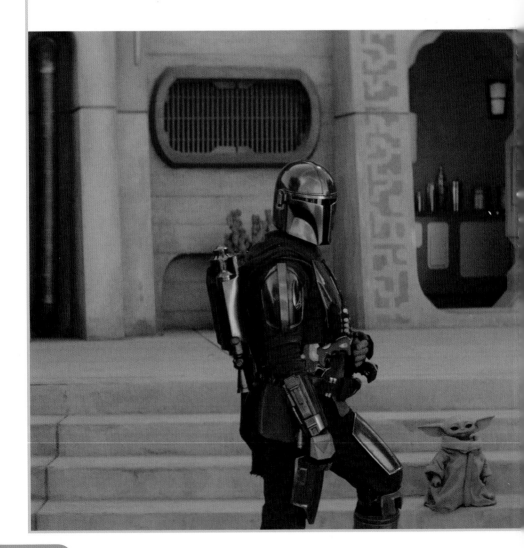

their ally Greef Karga on Nevarro. Greef gives them a cabin to live in between missions. Din Djarin and Grogu's adventures are not over yet!

Glossary

allies
people who help another person when they need it

astromech
an astromech droid is a type of droid that helps people travel around the galaxy

Bounty Hunters Guild
a group of bounty hunters who follow a number of rules

cabin
a type of house that is often small

cargo hold
a part of a vehicle from where items can be packed away

cockpit
a part of a starship where the pilot can control the vehicle

creature
another word for an animal

droid
another word for a robot

hover pram
a type of vehicle that can fly in the air and carries infants

mechanic
a person who helps build and repair machines

species
a type of living thing

starfighter
a type of starship often used in battle

starship
a type of vehicle that can travel in space

Index

Quiz

What have you learned about Din Djarin and his allies?

1. Who is Din Djarin's son?

2. Where does beskar come from?

3. Is the Armorer a Mandalorian?

4. R5-D4 is not an astromech droid. True or false?

5. Who helps Din Djarin on the planet Trask?

1. Grogu 2. Mandalore 3. Yes 4. False 5. Bo-Katan Kryze